Ripples

—A BOOK OF STORIES—

Dr. Latha Venkateswaran

BlueRose ONE .com
Stories Matter

First Published in June 2023

ISBN: 978-93-5741-401-2

BLUEROSE PUBLISHERS

www.BlueRoseONE.com

info@bluerosepublishers.com

+91 8882 898 898

Cover Design:

Tahira

Typographic Design:

Tanya Raj Upadhyay

Distributed by: BlueRose, Amazon, Flipkart

Preface

The world as we know it will henceforth be known as pre-COVID and post-COVID. It created a havoc of such mammoth proportions, that one simply couldn't ignore it. To me personally, though, it led to the creation of RIPPLES. I sincerely thank all who have helped me in this journey.

Firstly, Dr. Santosh Bharathan, my dear friend and classmate. His constant support was definitely the singular reason why RIPPLES saw the light of day. My thanks also to my editor, Lakshmi Venkatesh, and the editorial team of blue rose publishers who went through the entire book with a hawk,s eye. Varsha R.K. and Prof Dr. R.Sekar, whose guidance took this book to a better level. I thank Sunny Venkatesh, for being my greatest critic. I feel humbled by the gesture of my dear friends and family, who have penned a few lines of appreciation. Thanks to all my readers whose constant encouragement helped me write better. Lastly, a big thanks to my husband, son, and daughter, who never once doubted that I could do this.

- Latha Venkateswaran

Table of Contents

Saying Goodbye

It was midnight. Dr. Sheela was awake, pacing up and down the hallway of her home. At the break of dawn, she had to leave. To a faraway land, she barely knew. She only knew she was wanted there for her skill as an eminent surgeon. Ever since she joined 'Medicine Without Frontiers', she was hardly home. She seemed to be happiest doing what she was good at, in places ravaged by both human conflict and nature's fury. Healing humans, both physically and mentally, was her forte – a role she did to perfection. She would gladly accept every assignment that came her way.

But this time, it was different. She was finding it very hard to say her goodbyes. Especially to him. She had first seen him a year ago. From the moment she set her eyes on him, she knew she was bonded to him for life. Nothing would take that away; at least for her. He would be celebrating his birthday next week. She would not be there physically to partake in that joy. Would he miss her? A question, the answer to which she would never know. She was still trying to read through his emotions and understand him. It had been less than a year and she barely knew him. What a beautiful year it had been though! Most of her time in his company, running to his every beck and call. She would gladly do that for eternity.

The year gone was indeed filled with so much joy, love, and happiness that it was difficult for her to break away from that. She walked stealthily into the bedroom to sneak a glance at him. He was sleeping so peacefully that something tugged at her heart just to see that. Would he miss her when she was gone? She knew she would be away for at least six months if not more. The perils of her kind of job were that she might never come back. She shuddered to think of that eventuality. Never being able to see him again. Would he even remember her, if that were to happen? Shaking away that thought, Dr. Sheela started packing her suitcase. At least that would distract her for the time being. She barely had a couple of hours before they would come to fetch her.

Soon it was six in the morning. Emotions aside, she was now ready both mentally and physically. She opened the door at the ring of the bell. Taking a moment away from her colleagues and dear friends who had just come in, she went to see him one last time, in a long time to come. Opening the bedroom door, she went close to him and gracefully picked up her one-year-old son in her arms, hugged him, kissed him, and said her final goodbye!

The Anniversary

It was a beautiful summer morning. The rising sun had filled the skies with a splash of vibrant colors, so pleasing to the eye, that one could not take their gaze away from that richness. The octogenarian couple sat on the porch of their home many years, soaking in the morning glory. They were waiting for the day to unfold. The week leading up to this day had indeed been hectic. Their children, all five of them, were in the house. That was somehow unusual, but of course, a treat. The special occasion of the day demanded that. For they were celebrating their seventy-fifth wedding anniversary!

A pandal was covering the courtyard to accommodate the guests, who would soon be arriving. Their home overlooked a few acres of mango orchards, all of which were carefully nurtured by the old man himself over years of toil and sweat. The couple had lived in this village their entire life. They were indeed an inspiration to the villagers, who revered and considered them nothing less than demigods. Their lives had been an example for others to emulate. In the quiet of the early morning, holding his wife's hand, the man took a few moments to reminisce about the past, to the time when he had first met her.

She was thirteen. He, only a year older, was a farm boy, working for her father. She would be mostly in the fields helping out the farmers and her father. He noticed how frisky she was; so much like the lamb she always had by her side. Though very young, he had decided he would move all mountains to marry her. Love had bloomed in the fields. The elders happily approved of their union. They tied the knot, on this very same day, seventy-five years ago. Those were the days when he did not have much money. Their country was under the tyranny of a foreign hand and war was looming at large. However, the newly-weds were very happy and in love. The young farm boy knew he had to work hard to give his best to the little girl who had become his life partner. He swore he would do that. Slowly and steadily, hard work paid off and the man indeed became financially successful, buying land after land. They built this beautiful house they now called 'The Nest'. Their family had grown too and before long, they were proud parents to five children- three beautiful girls and two loving boys. Each one is so unique, but together they could pack a punch! Although the couple had no formal education, they made sure their children had the best. Their eldest was a daughter, who was so close to the mother, she continued living in the village and was a pillar of strength to them. The second, a son, was a very successful lawyer who did many good things for the people and the community he lived in. Their third and fourth, were daughters, one an artist and the other a doctor, and both good in their respective fields. Their youngest was their surprise. He was a successful actor, a superstar, and the entire village considered him their very own. All except for him were happily married and between them had seven children. 'Had it really been that many years', wondered the old man. It seemed like yesterday.

A sudden din brought him back to the present. The household was waking. The grandchildren were running around, not heeding the call of the couple. The guests were trickling in. Their children greeted them at the door and made them comfortable. The couple tried to engage in the animated chatter that filled their home, but nobody seemed to mind them. Even the eldest daughter seemed a wee bit distracted, not really talking much to the mother. Closer to the designated time for the ceremonies, the priests arrived. By then, the courtyard was filling up. The villagers started gathering too. The couple looked proudly at the arrangements made by their children. They had done it all, without really troubling them. Before long, the ceremonies were ready to start. As the priest called out to their eldest son to offer prayers to the departed souls, the siblings couldn't fight back their tears! And they heard one of the guests saying "What a noble couple they were! It is indeed sad we lost them this day, last year. Even in death, they were together. That too on the very day they got married, and even if they are not physically present today, I am sure they are here, amongst us, in spirit!"

The Intrusion

There were nights when Anne just couldn't sleep. She was the district's very efficient public prosecutor. Her job meant putting many high profile people behind bars and

therefore making enemies more often than not. In court, she would seldom give a chance for the defendant's lawyer to have the upper hand, winning almost all of the cases hands down. Outside of all that, she was the loving wife of an equally famous psychiatrist and a doting mother to a very energetic seven-year-old. Settling in the suburbs was their choice. They had a sprawling villa tucked away in theGreenlands of the city. Their nearest neighbour was about a kilometer away. She loved the area and the solitude it offered, but on the days her husband was away at a conference or meeting, she would always have the jitters.

This was one such day. It had been exhausting for her. The defending lawyer had torn apart her client, a twenty-year-old girl, who had suffered brutal assault at the hands of her tormentor. But she didn't want to think about that. She was relaxing in their bedroom upstairs. Dinner was done, and their son was asleep next door. The help had left for the day. Her husband was away attending a conference, leaving the two of them alone. There was an eerie silence that enveloped the evening. She had already spoken on the phone to her husband, updating him on the day's events. She missed him even though he was gone only a day. Time seemed to tick away slowly, making her restless.

Suddenly, she heard a noise at the front door, as if someone were trying to open it. She made a mental check. She had locked the door and set the alarm. She reached out to her bag and took the pepper spray out. Immediately her thoughts were to safeguard her son. Quietly she walked out of her room, towards her son's bedroom. Just then the lights all went out. She has her phone with her and saw that there was no signal. She was about to dial the emergency, when she heard a loud bang, and the front door give way. Her son started to scream and instantly she knew they were in trouble. She quickly ran to fetch her son, gathered, him, and stood behind the bedroom door, one hand firmly on his mouth. The stranger came barging into the room. Armed with the pepper spray, she used it liberally onto his eyes and ran out and down into the kitchen leaving him screaming for mercy. She noticed that he was wielding a knife. Hiding her son in the closet by the dining area and telling him to remain quiet, she ran towards the kitchen counter and picked up the carving knife. It was still very dark. She remained extremely quiet and prayed that her son would do so too. She could hear the man come down the stairs. His steps were loud and angered. He slipped down a few steps, steadied himself, and made his way straight at her. The darkness played to her advantage as she knew her way around. The silence was overpowering as both were readying their moves. Anne was firm that she would do something only if confronted directly. At that very moment, she heard the swoosh of the knife close to her left elbow and directly plunged the carver in that direction. She heard the man scream. With all her strength, she drove the knife right into him and felt the splatter of blood hit her face. The man's body went limp and fell with a thud on the floor. Her son came crying from the closet and she hugged him. In the distance, she could hear the sirens and hoped they were coming toward her house. Terrified at the events of the evening and happy it all ended, she finally got her breath!

"Are we done yet?" asked Jane's husband, peeping into her study. "Hmm. Think I can say yes", she replied. Not easy being an author, she thought. She had been working on this story since dawn. Although it still needed a lot of editing, she felt good about it now. Closing her computer, she got up, stretched herself, gave her husband a loving peck on his cheek, and went on to get ready for the dinner date the two had planned that evening.

The Journey

Atman was ecstatic. He was finally going on that journey he kept talking about for quite some time now. He knew it was a perilous one, though at the same time, spiritual too. He

was told that it would take him roughly ten to fifteen days to reach his destination. So many things to be arranged before that. Firstly, once there, he had to decide whether he would ever come back. Leaving behind his family and friends was not something he looked forward to. However, his wife was already there and she seemed happy. He missed her and wanted to join her. She would send messages occasionally telling him how content she was. Which was why, despite his frail body, he was willing to take the risk of the journey. He had talked to a lot of his peers over the last few months. They also seemed to have the same desire. Finally, it was happening.

It was the 1800s. His family traded in chintz, which was a kind of cotton weave. It was used for almost every item of clothing. His was a large joint family, almost all of them actively involved in the flourishing textile industry of the century. Despite oppression and continued antagonism against the making of any indigenous product imposed upon the foreign rulers, they were somehow comfortable.

His children were all married and well-settled. He knew he could go peacefully and that the time was right.

Leaving behind a well-earned legacy, he set on his journey that wonderful day. His family had gathered to say their goodbyes. There were a lot of tears shed and plenty of hugs. His grandchildren kept asking why he had to leave. . But he knew he had to! They had packed a sumptuous meal and plenty of water. He would walk his way. A lamp was also given enough oil to keep it burning. With a stick in hand, a good pair of slippers, a brolly to beat the heat and rain and, for some strange reason, a cow for the company, he set foot.

Days went by. Somehow, he was able to cope. Crisscrossing areas of large forests interspersed with arid regions he moved on. Food and water seemed to not be a grave problem. He always got enough of it whenever he wanted, although he was seldom hungry or thirsty. He was, of course, joined by many. Some were very old, others not so. He also noticed that not all of them made the cut. Despite help from all around, some of them just succumbed to the perils. Or so he thought.. With every passing day, some whom he'd met earlier, were no longer seen or heard of.

Around the twelfth day came the most dangerous part of the journey. They had heard about it. A large river to be crossed. Their destination was on the other side of this magnificent stretch of water. Almost twenty miles of it. They had to leave behind everything before the cross. Atman was ready. He said his goodbye to the loving cow who had never left his side and, in fact, nudged him to take the boat. He gave the boatman his coin and all along the boat ride, kept chatting to his ferrier about his life and its many important milestones. As they cruised along, the river took a sharp turn in its course leading to a large fall. It was do or die.

He could see a lot of boats toppling over. Atman said his prayers as he felt the boat take the plunge.

That was it. His life had suddenly brought him to his final destination. As if waking from a trance, he adjusted his vision and could see, in the distance, a shimmering light and many familiar voices. He filtered them, to hear the one voice he so badly wanted to hear! The beautiful call of his dear wife! Filled with joy he walked towards her and the light. Finally, his journey complete, Atman knew he had merged with the *Paramatman*!

The Birth

Rosie stood outside the gates of the palatial house she had once called home. It was raining incessantly since the break of dawn and she was drenched to her bones. She

looked longingly inside, through the grill, hoping to catch the attention of the sentry who always stood to guard right there. Would he even recognize her in that state? Was it really two years since she had left home and everyone who loved her so much? It was a decision she would look back on with regret each time the harsh world outside meted its cruelty on her. A flood of emotions filled her as she recollected the day she had stomped out in a frenzy! Her father was not in a good mood that ill-fated day. She had crossed his path the wrong way and he had been nasty to her. That was when she had just walked out, leaving all that was hitherto precious to her far behind. She had been confident then, but life taught her otherwise.

The streets were not made for someone of her kind. Although she had borne it with some dignity initially, things were getting much worse for her now. She soon realized that the sanctity and safety of her home were irreplaceable. She could take no more. She wanted to be back home again. She was drenched, tired, weak, and above all ... very pregnant!!!

As she stood there almost fainting, the gates opened and she heard her name being called. “ROSIE”, the watchman squealed as soon as he saw her! He wasted no time in summoning everyone outside. Suddenly, the entire household came alive and within no time, they were all at the gate. Her parents, and siblings, were all so emotionally charged and unable to contain their happiness on seeing her. The questions started pouring in and all she could do was remain speechless and hang her head in shame. Michael, her brother, to whom she was the closest, did not waste any more time taking her in. They saw how much she had withered. She heard her mother tell the cooks to prepare her favorite meal. Once she had eaten, she was taken to her room which was exactly how she had left it. Her bed was made and they told her to rest. She was so happy that they welcomed her with open arms!

The next few weeks went by like a breeze. Considering her current state, she was taken to the doctor at the earliest. Apart from being weak, the doctor announced that all seemed well with Rosie and her baby. From then on, regular visits to the doctor, good food, lots of rest, and loads of love, saw Rosie glow once again. She regained her strength and cheer. She no longer felt abandoned. Long evening walks with Michael made her strong and able. He was always by her side, tending to her every need! And she was so thankful for that.

Soon it was time. The baby was coming. The entire family was prepared to welcome the little one into their lives! Being very influential, the family was able to convince the doctor for home delivery. The doctor did oblige and was in attendance along with her assistants. Despite everyone telling him to, Michael refused to leave her side. He could not bear to see her going through the ordeal all by herself with only strangers around. Nothing prepared Rosie for what she was about to experience in the next few hours! Sometimes hollering and sometimes whimpering, she bore the pain of labor. Michael was there, holding her, talking to her, helping her withstand it all.

Almost four hours later, an ecstatic Michael came screaming out of the room and exclaimed: "Mom, Dad, we have four beautiful puppies! And Rosie is fine too!" A lot of prayers were chanted. Within no time, the entire family gathered around Rosie and her litter. She looked at her pups with pride and licked them lovingly! Exhausted, but content that her babies were in a safe haven; she closed her eyes and went off to sleep.

The Conquest

Shaurya was going to be twenty-one soon. She knew it would be a special day in her life. For almost six months now, she had been training herself. Her aim was to conquer the mighty Himalayas, more specifically the Everest. All 8848 meters of it. It was not unusual to have such a dream for someone born into a family of Sherpas.

She had lived on the foothills of the Himalayas all her life. The magnificent mountains were the first thing she would witness every morning. Her father and brothers were guides, helping the many enthusiastic mountaineers scale the heights. Every time she told her father that she too wanted to do so, he would somehow find an excuse to steer her off. But now, she would no longer take no for an answer. She was determined. This year, nothing would stop her.

For the last four months, she had kept to a very rigid routine. Her day would begin at four a.m., much before the sun would peep from the summit of the mountain she wanted to conquer. The mountains were almost paternal to her. Watching her, teasing her, sympathizing with her.

On waking, she would first head to the monastery for the day's blessings. Once done, she would start her intense training. Trekking for an hour or more with the gear she eventually would carry on her way to the top. Then sprinting for another hour. Being born and raised at high altitudes, acclimatization was not so much of a problem for her. Nevertheless, the three hours or so of the morning routine would completely exhaust her. However, she kept at it every single day. In the evenings when the family gathered for dinner, her father would counsel her on the many perils that could befall her on the journey. She would just listen in silence and nod her head. Nothing would stop her now.

Finally, it was the day to start. The journey would last for ten days. They would halt at four camps before making the final climb. Their group consisted of her brother and eight other Sherpas. No one was inexperienced. Her father wanted only the best of escorts for his dear daughter. Shaurya was excited! She was awake an hour earlier that day. She had readied her gear and some imperishable food that her mother had lovingly packed. It was important to take only what was most essential. Like every day, she first went to the monastery and spent a good fifteen minute in silent prayer. The group joined her too and sort blessings for a successful climb. Soon they were on their way! Slowly and steadily, they went from camp to camp. It was day eight. They were at the last campsite, sipping tea. No amount of training actually helped the challenges Shaurya had to face to reach this far. The harsh terrain, the blinding snow, the many steep climbs, and the frostbite, all took their toll on her physical and mental strength. She looked at the mountains all around and prayed to them "Take care of me. Be with me. Just get me there." she muttered silently.

Finally, it was the last climb of around a thousand meters. With the cold wind blowing into them like a jagged knife, the group trudged along. The Sherpas were only too eager to render any help to her, but she was determined to do this on her own as much as possible. It was almost nightfall and their aim was to reach the summit before that. The air was thinning, breathing was an exercise in itself and what was left was the very last hundred meters before the top. Shaurya walked on courageously holding on to the tight rope that they had tied around themselves for an easier climb. As the last rays of the sun were disappearing into the vast horizon, her brother suddenly exclaimed that they were already there! Shaurya was speechless. The mountain overwhelmed her. Tired and exhausted, they pitched their makeshift tents and called it a day.

Daybreak came too soon. It was Shaurya's twenty first birthday. She had done it! Her brother and others came up to her, wished her, and congratulated her on her achievement. It was indeed remarkable. She thanked them all wholeheartedly and shared the homemade cake her mother had lovingly packed. She then looked around at the vastness that engulfed her. Was that it? Perhaps so. Sore on her knees, Shaurya then cheerfully picked up the pair of artificial legs and fitted them on with pride, reflecting a moment on the cruel accident that had costed her both her legs at the tender age of fifteen, while trying to climb the very mountain she stood on top of now. However, she never once stopped believing in herself. She only became stronger and more determined in her desire to conquer the mighty Himalayas. She had now done it and that felt ecstatic. Brushing the thought aside, she was now ready to start her descent!

Fear

Prologue

LOLA was a nightbird. She was at her best then. She enjoyed working the night shift at the all-night diner. It paid her tuition and she met a lot of new folks with varied interests and stories. She usually finished her shift around five in the morning. During the winter months, daybreak would be late and the streets were dark. Many mornings she would find herself walking back home in pitch darkness, with only a few streetlights to help find her way. It was one such morning. She handed over the cash from the counter to her colleague and was walking back to her studio apartment, the rent for which came from the job. The street soon gave way to a dark alley. As she walked ahead, she could hear the growls of the strays. She immediately became alert. At a distance, the canines had gathered around a dumpster and were ferociously staring at something. Cautiously, she walked towards that. Reaching close enough to see, she let out a shrill scream. There, lying amongst the garbage was a man, his torso exposed, a pool of blood beside his legs which were distorted out of shape. His eyes were gouged out. A few teeth lay scattered around him. Then, something unusual caught Lola's attention. She leaned forward to see and let out yet another scream. Carved on his torso in his own blood was the number five. He had long been dead.

Chapter One

Hamish McCallum was a family man. He would rather spend time in the company of his wife and children than anywhere else. But he seldom had that luxury. Being the chief detective of the precinct, he was at his work almost always. A brawl outside a pub between rival gangs had left one of them stabbed. The incident had kept him there a good part of the night, trying to sort things out. With a few arrests made and the wounded sent to hospital, he had returned home only at six A.M.

It was a glorious Monday morning. As he made his way to the kitchen, he saw his wife of fifteen years, Akila, coming down the stairs and into the kitchen. She was the lead and head of the department of psychiatry at the district hospital.

They had met at work, which soon blossomed into care and respect, eventually into love and a winter wedding. Their strong bond was sealed by the extended love of two children. Every time he saw her, his heart skipped a beat and he kept reminding himself how lucky he was. "Good morning dear," she said" long night?". "It could've been worse" he replied. "Oh, do tell me. I had one of those weird nights too. I came in only at two." "What happened?" he questioned. "Paramedics brought in a thirty-something woman who was in a state of catatonic seizure. She was stabilized and sedated in the ER. She was found at the ER entrance. We still have no ID. There were signs of minor assault on her, mostly defensive and superficial. She hasn't said a word since admission.The attending physician has asked me to consult. I will have to go back soon. Will you drive the boys to school today?" She barely said the word and their boys were down in the kitchen.

Shiv was eight and Noah, six. Handsome youngsters blessed with the blend of two cultural identities in their genes. Akila was a devout Hindu and Hamish loved that. She made sure the boys imbibed that culture too. "Morning mom, dad" the kids echoed. "Breakfast ready guys!" said Akila as she pecked them both on their cheeks. "Mom..." whined Shiv as if all grown up. Shiv was into theatre and he had an important play coming up. Noah was the sportsman. Still not sure what his calling was. At that moment, he was sliding toward gymnastics. "Your father will take you to school, kids", Akila said. "Dad, don't forget I have theatre group this evening. You need to come an hour late to pick me up", said Shiv straight away. "And what about you, young man?" Hamish turned to Noah. At that very moment, his phone rang, disturbing the morning banter of the family. Reluctantly he answered. "Hello David", he said replying to his junior's call. Soon the playful expression on his face changed to grim and he kept nodding. "Right, I will be there shortly. Give me fifteen" he said and hung up. Turning to his family he said "Ok off we go boys. Got a homicide on the precinct. No time to waste."

Chapter Two

Two decades earlier...

The girls were terrified. There were five of them. Still pressed to the corner of a dingy darkroom, reeking of bodily excretions. Extreme fear was the only emotion they had known right from a very young age. They were unsure when they had been put in the room. But they dreaded the monster who did that and knew he would soon be there. Greta was the strongest. She kept the others sane and took most of the beating and torture vetted upon them. She would constantly reassure Lisa, Dolly, Eve, and Maria that she would definitely find a way out for all of them. They were all around the age of ten. They either had no family or did not know they had one. They saw only the one man who had total control of their life and hoped and prayed that things would get better someday. Lisa had vague memories of her mom, whom she remembered was kind and gentle. Going to school with her, and enjoying the evenings in her company, she always looked forward to the stories her mom would read to her every night before bed. She did not know her father.

Then that dreadful night, this monster had barged into the house from nowhere, beat her mother to near death, and taken Lisa away. That was the last time Lisa saw her mother. She was held prisoner ever since. She had no recollection of when the other girls had joined her or from where, but they held on to each other and endured every passing day in fear.

Food was given to them when the man felt like it. Most days they were hungry. Water was scarce. They treasured what little was provided to them like gold. They were all malnourished. But Greta kept them sane and they all looked up to her for solace. Days passed into months and perhaps, months into years. They knew that, as they had lost a few teeth and grown taller and leaner.

This day was special. Greta had told them they would leave that room once and for all. Over the years, the girls had struggled to dig out parts of the wall with their bare hands, keeping it well hidden from the eyes of the man. Most days he would come in drunk and find some excuse to beat one of them. But though exhausted and sad always, Greta never let go of the hope. Every single day they did some digging. The room had one window. Nothing else. One cot with a sheet, where all of them cuddled. A toilet with little or no water at the other end. That was part of the room which had loose flooring, where the girls had started tunnelling. The man was out of the room for the day. Lisa, the most fragile of the girls had taken the brunt of his anger this time. But the moment he was gone, Greta wasted no time in huddling the girls. She wiped the tears from Lisa's face and sent them down the tunnel. Almost half a kilometer long, dark, and narrow, they kept going. Their fingers were half eaten from all the digging over the years, but it did not matter anymore. Freedom was a few steps away now. Greta had known that from the last digging. They had reached the surface and she could feel that. They kept moving, afraid to look back. Finally, they were at the end of the tunnel, where, talking animatedly and all together, they took turns clawing away at the earth. As if on cue, the ground gave way at one place.

They wasted no time. With tears of joy covering their faces, huddled and crying, they finally emerged out into freedom, so cruelly taken away from them for many years. It was a bright sunny day. Something the girls hadn't experienced in that hellhole. They ran as fast as their strength would allow and finally screamed and lunged their way into the arms of a young lady walking her dog.

Chapter Three

Current day

"What do we have here?" asked Hamish as he walked straight into David Miller, his close confidante and partner at work. Though much junior to Hamish, David had picked up the nuances of dealing with crime in a very short span of time. Hamish liked him and felt lost when he was not around. "Unidentified man found dead, by the lady there". David replied pointing to Lola who still looked shell shocked. "She works at the diner two blocks away. She was returning home after her night shift. The call came around five thirty a.m". No murder weapon or weapons found anywhere." "Hmm" said Hamish. "What does it look like" he asked. "Forensics at a glance said death could have been between eleven P.M. and two A.M. The body is reeking of alcohol. Someone has really worked on him. Guess he was too weak and intoxicated to resist. Name's Arthur Scott as per a trucker's driving license found on him. Doesn't seem to be a local. Could've been passing by" filled in David. "Good work young man" Hamish said giving him a pat. A small crowd had gathered. The police had cordoned off the crime scene. Press was eager to get their share of the story. Forensics were trying to gather all that could be obtained. "Let's get the body to the autopsy table at the earliest" he said and went to talk to a petrified Lola.

"Morning Rita", said Akila to the head nurse of her department as she walked into the ward. "How are we today?"

“Your Jane Doe hasn't still said a word nor eaten anything” said Rita without even bothering to exchange morning pleasantries.

She was efficient and all about work “Ok. Let’s see what I can do” said Akila. Practicing psychiatry could be stressful. Often it required breaking into the closed soul of the individual. Akila’s compassion and patience made her good at it. Despite being in her forties, she had come up the ranks in good time. As she took her strides towards the morning rounds, Rita followed her. After efficiently dealing with her regulars, she walked into the room of the lady admitted the night before. “Morning dear”, she said. She was met with a cold stare. “Did you sleep well?” a question to which the answer was obvious. The breakfast tray was untouched. Akila turned toward Rita, who on cue, walked away. “What shall I call you? You are welcome to take your time but I am here to help you. I know we do not provide the best food but you also need to eat something” she said nudging the breakfast tray toward her. She tried to converse but there seemed to be a wall staring back at he. After more than fifteen minutes of getting nowhere, Akila said “Ok then, I will come back in the noon.” As she was stepping out, she heard a faint voice say “Lisa”. Quickly she walked back to her, sat by her side, and said “Hello Lisa. I am Akila, your friend for today”. Tears streaming out, Lisa leaned over and laid her head on Akila's shoulder.

Chapter Four

Lisa walked into her class. She loved being amongst children. Teaching them art was even more enjoyable. Art was her passion. She was quite well-known in art circles for her work. The pictures she made, depicted a lot of melancholy and angst. Though she had made good money through her passion, she wanted to give back something to society. Which is why she volunteered to teach art at her local school twice a week. Her students were fourth graders, taking baby steps in the world of art. “Good morning, all” she greeted them. “Morning Miss Hayden” the children replied. “I have a masterpiece for you to replicate today,” she said opening a picture of a train making its way across a bridge over a river roaring with fullness and meandering around a valley. Let’s paint this today, shall we?” she queried. “Yes, Miss Hayden” the children echoed and gleefully got on to it. Looking at them lost in their handiwork, she thought there was potential here. It only needed tapping. Her thoughts went back to her childhood. She shuddered at that memory. Many innocent years were snatched away by a cruel man. But she had grown stronger since and pursued her passion. It had been two decades since her freedom.

Police gathered around the dilapidated house as soon as they could. It was a quiet neighbourhood with mostly young families occupying the modest row houses. All, except this one. Not maintained very well, and the people around always wondered who the owner was. But no one really bothered to find out. They seldom noticed any activity in the house. It seemed that the only occupant was a man in his thirties. He was quiet and moved in and out mostly at night. The lady walking the dog was aghast at the turn of events that morning and had quickly called the police. The girl seemed to come from the direction of that house and soon the police had zeroed in on the man. He was arrested and a lot of evidence was gathered. The inside of the house was as illmaintained as the outside. The basement bore witness to the years of suffering. The walls of the basement, however, were testimony of a free-spirited life in captivity. It was decorated with drawings mainly done with stones, depicting the sun, faces, birds, and the like.

Lisa, as she was known after she was free, was adopted by an elderly childless couple, whose care and love had helped her bloom into a beautiful young lady and become Lisa Hayden. Her parents, who had given her a home and name, were now no more. She had a boyfriend for three years who was a businessman and an art lover, whom she had met at one of her exhibitions. He had fallen in love with both her and her creations. He knew her past and helped her cope with it. She still had sessions with her psychiatrist and continued meeting her friends from the days of her captivity, albeit of late, only occasionally.

Chapter Five

The autopsy room of the district hospital was a neatly kept quadrant, authoritatively ruled by a rather pudgy lady called Dr. Camilla Baron. Hamish and David walked into the room to find her hands very busy working on the body of the man found dead in the early hours of that morning. "Good morning Dr. Baron" Hamish greeted her. "Hello, you two" she replied. "Almost done here. No surprises. A fatal blow on the occiput is the cause of death, most likely around one A.M. His eyes were gouged out before death. Another blow over the legs has left them both shattered. Internal organs seem ok. However, he has alcohol levels in his blood that are beyond reason. Could've been drinking the whole evening. Some undigested food in his stomach. I have sent samples to the lab. Also asked for DNA testing. Will take a week or so given our budget. He probably did not put up much of a fight." "Well thank you!" Hamish replied as he walked toward the autopsy table hand over his nose. "Will wait to hear from you with more details". As he turned away Dr. Baron added, "Oh yes I also found a strand of hair in his nails. Probably the attackers. Have sent that to the lab too." "Great," he said. "Let's get cracking, shall we?"

"Did you find anything on Arthur Scott in our database, David?" "Well it appears that name could be an alias. The address on the license we found on him is almost a five-hour drive from here. No insurance or social security number". "I think we have to take that drive then," said Hamish "and of course wait for the DNA results."

Akila was in her ward for the evening rounds. “You ought to go in there,” said Rita as soon as she saw her. “You mean Lisa?” asked Akila. “Who else?” said Rita frowning a bit. With the in-patient chart in her hand and checking the medications, Akila walked into Lisa's room. Lisa had eaten some lunch and slept the whole afternoon.

As she walked into the room, she heard someone say “Hello you must be Akila. I am Greta, Lisa's friend. “Oh! Hello. Yes I am Dr. Akila McCallum.” said Akila quite surprised. “She hasn't said much, has she?” asked Greta. “That’s correct, so what happened? You seem to have some bruising too.” “It’s nothing. We girls were having a night out and had to ward off a drunken group of noisy guys on our way out.” “I see,” said Akila. “But we found Lisa almost unconscious near the ER.” “I don't know. We said our goodbyes a little after midnight and then went our way.” said Greta. “Hmm,” said Akila. “So what do you do Greta? And where does Lisa live?” “I teach self-defense to children at the community centre. Don’t ask me where she lives. We never meet in our houses.” “So, do you know her family?” “She lives alone but has a boyfriend whom I don’t see.” “Why is that?” retorted Akila. “Oh! that’s just the way it is. We girls keep our lives separate.” said Greta. “Girls?” asked Akila, eyebrows raised. “Yes, we are a strong group. You will meet the others too soon enough.” “Would love to” said Akila. “Well, I’ll be on my way then! See you around!” said Greta leaving as quickly as she could. “Lisa?” said Akila. Lisa looked in her direction said nothing and closed her eyes as if done for the day.

Chapter Six

Hamish and David were on the road. David was driving. Hamish was enjoying the country music playing on his partner's music system. 'Country music tells stories' he thought as the morning sun started becoming brighter. They had another hour to reach the address of the deceased. Not much conversation. Just the music and a long winding road. Hardly any traffic except for the occasional trucker. Soon they were at the place. A modest neighbourhood in the hinterlands of the country. They reached the building housing the apartment and found that it was bustling with activity. Parking the car, they walked toward the main entrance of the building and started their inquiries. Arthur Scott had rented the apartment a year ago, was hardly around, and paid the rent in cash. Seemed like a dead end. The apartment he rented was opened for them to see. They found a truck company's brochure whose office was close by. They decided to go there and seek some answers.

Akila walked into the ward and Rita filled her up with the day's news. "During the initial assessment of Lisa in ER, they found some blood and skin tissue on Lisa's nails. The lab called today to inform us that the sample was not hers. They have sent the samples to the genetic lab for DNA testing." "That's informative" Akila replied. "Her fingertips seemed to be chewed up, from years of some kind of insult. What did she do? Also, I am sure she has a therapist in the city. Can you dig that out?" "Sure," said Rita. "And oh! There is someone else in the room now. Good luck!" "Thank you. Much needed" replied Akila and walked into Lisa's room.

"Good morning. Whom do we have here today?" "Hello there. Lisa has mentioned you a lot in the last two days." "Is that so? And you must be..." "Oh! I am Eve, Lisa's friend." "Of course, you are. And what do you do?" "I am a teacher too. I teach mathematics. Same school as Lisa. Twice a week" she replied. "Which school is that? And do you know where Lisa lives? Haven't been able to trace that. How did you two meet?" "We have known each other since we were ten. I need to go now" said Eve abruptly. "Well thank you for coming by," said Akila. She then addressed Lisa who had gotten off the cot. "Are you ok?" "I feel terribly tired," said Lisa. "Do you remember what led you to come here?" "No, I just remember we were out having fun. My head hurts. Can I rest please?" she pleaded. "Sure!", said Akila.

Walking back to the nursing station, Akila held the file and told Rita "there are three of them now" "Yes" replied Rita. "Could you call the psychiatry practices in the vicinity and check whether Lisa was enrolled anywhere?"

Hamish and Akila had just finished dinner with their boys. They were ready to call it a day. Both of them had had a difficult day. "Not really getting anywhere with that murder of two days ago," said Hamish. "The name's an alias and not in any of our databases. We drove five hours to check at the address on his license. Not much luck there too. He was employed as a truck driver and may have driven into our city recently." "I have had quite the day myself. Trying to figure out the woman who came in a couple of nights ago. Interesting turn of events there. Still no trace of her whereabouts" she said, as she switched the lights off.

Chapter Seven

Hamish was disturbed at the turn of events. He was getting nowhere. Normally he would have some insight into the crime within a couple of days, but here he was- lost. He decided to take another look at the crime scene. It was quite early in the day. He walked around the dumpsters looking to see if he could find anything. The strays were all around sniffing and snarling. Since the area was cordoned off from the public till further notice, the garbage lay undisturbed from the day the body was discovered. As he moved a few bags around with his feet, he heard metal creaking on gravel. Looking further into that spot he soon found a phone. The screen was completely shattered. With gloved hands, he picked it up and bagged it.

Mark Webster landed at JFK airport a little after twelve noon. He had had a successful business trip lasting a week and was now looking forward to unwinding at home, with his girlfriend. He called her from the airport but her phone was switched off. 'Strange' he thought. He had not been able to reach her for the past three days. He got into a taxi and found his way home. Opening the doors, he walked straight into the kitchen. It appeared unused. He put on the answering machine and found the messages were not heard, including his, from the previous day. Tired to think more about that, he took a shower and crashed into bed.

Akila was in the ward at nine in the morning. She went into her office and her secretary came in with some coffee. "There is a Lisa Hayden listed in Dr. Dorothy Parker's practice. Five miles from here" she said, placing the coffee on the table. "I know Dotty. Get her on the phone will you? Let's see if it is indeed the Lisa, we have with us." said Akila. "Already did. Dr. Dorothy is away at a conference and is expected to be at work on Friday." "Oh. That's two days later." sighed Akila.

Hamish found David in the office, surrounded by a set of files. He walked in and handed over the phone. "Found this at the crime scene. How did they miss it?" he asked. "Could you get this working, please? Ask our tech department. Fingerprints need to be traced too." "Sure", said David as he took the bag with the phone.

The day was closing in. Mark woke up as if in a trance. Looking at the clock he realised he had slept for six hours straight. He called his girlfriend's phone, but it was still switched off. 'Where are you Lisa?' he thought.

Chapter Eight

(A few days earlier...)

Lisa liked to shop on her own. Her boyfriend was impatient and she did not like that. She liked to spend time at the supermarket, look at the offers going on and buy at leisure. She usually did that after school on Fridays.

It was crowded that evening. She had shopped for dinner hoping to cook a lovely meal. Her boyfriend was away on a business trip and sometimes she enjoyed an evening to herself. She joined the other shoppers in one of the lines leading to the cash counter. Suddenly there was a commotion at one of the counters. The cashier and an elderly man were arguing. As she moved forward in her line, she saw the face of the man who was arguing. She almost fainted. It was him. Undoubtedly, the man of her nightmares. She left all that was in the trolley and ran out as if she'd seen a ghost in broad daylight and she indeed had. 'I must tell the girls' she thought to herself.

The next couple of days, unknown to him, the girls followed him. He was staying in a motel. He was driving a truck and had made many deliveries over the days. Evenings he spent at the diner, drinking for more than four hours and leaving around midnight.

It was a Sunday evening. The girls had followed him to the diner. They sat well away from his sight and were watching him. He was at his eighth drink and quite tipsy. Around midnight he left the diner and started walking in the direction of the alley. It was very dark. Lisa followed. Soon, Greta, Eve, Maria, and Dolly joined her.

Lisa had a carving knife in her hand. Greta picked up a metal rod from the construction site nearby. They closed in on him. As he heard the footsteps, he turned back. Quite intoxicated to resist, he took the first blow on his feeble legs. They shattered at the impact. He fell with a thud. Eve and Dolly gouged his eyes out. Greta wrote the number five on his torso, with the blood that was pouring out of him. Lisa then took the rod and landed a powerful blow on his skull, silencing his screams forever.

Then, as if in a trance, Lisa picked up the rod and the knife, ran in the direction of the canal nearby, and threw them into it. She then turned back and made her way to the hospital ER. It was around one a.m. by then. Reaching the hospital, she collapsed in a state of catatonic seizure.

Chapter Nine

It was Thursday morning. Mark was ready early in the day. He tried reaching Lisa on the phone and it was still switched off. He decided to go to her school and ask around. He reached the school and went straight to the principal's chamber. He was told that she had not come in since Monday. They too had been trying to reach out to her. Disappointed, he then went to her taekwondo class and enquired. They hadn't seen her either. He thought that it was time to seek help from the police. He called her phone once again and this time it did ring.

Hamish was in his office when David barged in and said "Two new developments. The phone you gave me, is now working. The team is answering the missed calls. It belongs to a lady who goes by the name of Lisa Hayden. Her boyfriend called a while ago and said she had been missing for three to four days. Also, a metal rod and knife were found in the canal by some men who were cleaning it. It's with the forensic team now. Could be the murder weapons." "That's an excellent development. We now need to find Lisa," replied Hamish.

Akila was in Lisa's room. She had got a call from the hospital at seven A.M., saying Lisa was turning violent and incoherent. She had rushed in as soon as she could. They were five of them now and all were talking simultaneously." "Lisa, you tell me what is happening," asked Akila trying to calm her. "She is not going to tell you anything," said Greta. "But I will After all, the truth will come out soon". "Yes" echoed Dolly, Maria, and Eve one after the other. “What do you want to tell me?” Akila queried. “I killed him”, said Greta. “He deserved to die!” “No, it was me!” Maria said. “What do you know about killing? I gouged his eyes out!” pitched in Eve. “And I helped you there” said Dolly. Lisa was silent. “Talk to me Lisa”, said Akila. At that moment, her secretary came into the room and announced “Dr. Dorothy Parker for you.” “I'll take that,” she said and called Rita into the room to sedate Lisa. She walked toward the phone, picked it up, and started listening to Dr. Dorothy Parker, Lisa's therapist.

Akila listened intently to Dr. Dorothy. After fifteen minutes she sighed and said “I see. You need to come here and at least talk to her. I have sedated her for now. But she should be awake in a couple of hours.”

Rita came out of Lisa's room. “How is she?” asked Akila. “She is sleeping. I had a call from the genetic lab. It is regarding Lisa's DNA results. They said it was urgent” Rita filled her in. Akila called them back. She was extremely surprised at what they told her. Disconnecting the phone, she immediately called her husband. Detective Hamish McCallum came straight away along with David. He was briefed by Akila about the turn of events and slowly walked into Lisa's room to find her fast asleep. Akila joined him inside. She looked at Lisa and told Hamish “Five tormented souls in one body. With regular therapy, Lisa had tried her best to keep the others dormant all these years. Just seeing the monster, has brought back all of them. She will need years of therapy to set it right again.” “Lisa!” they heard someone call. Both of them turned back to see Mark Webster standing at the door.

Epilogue

Over the next few days, the team connected the missing dots. A wider search of the dead man's DNA result had found a match. It was that of a prisoner who had served twenty years for unlawful confinement and negligence of his daughter. He was out on parole and working as a truck driver.

The daughter, Lisa Hayden, had shown all signs of dissociative identity disorder, commonly known as split personality, at the time of her escape from her father. There were definitely five different personas residing in her. It was as if the five elements: air, water, wind, earth, and sky, (*panchabhootam*) were within her. With therapy, she had become better, and kept them under control, until the fateful day she saw the man who had kept her captive for so many years. Given the right moment, the five had become a violent force of nature, overwhelming her, and killing him without any remorse.

The murder weapons were confirmed to be those found in the canal. They had Lisa's fingerprints on them. She would go on trial for murder once the formalities were complete and presented to the court. In the meantime, Akila continued to support and care for Lisa who had known only one strong emotion most of her life - that of FEAR!

The Assassin

Prologue

The mercenary had chosen his spot. His target was 1000 yards away. Days of planning and studying his target's movements had preceded his decision of committing the act on this day. He was always patient before any kill. Much like the tiger awaits its prey. Sometimes it would take him just a few days in planning. Sometimes months. Nevertheless, he seldom hurried to get things done. A perfectionist, he would wait for as long as it would take him to do it without failing. His clients were high-profile members of the society. There was no dearth of money in his line of work. However, in every assignment, he had the final say. He would plan the whole thing. No one was allowed access to his modus operandi. Those who availed of his services barely knew him, nor could they contact him directly. It was only through middlemen and each time it was a different person. They would hear from him, only when the job was done. He was very private, never used the same identity twice, had a slew of facial camouflage and seldom made for good company. Once his work was done he would disappear without a trace. The pay was good and he nursed no remorse after, as he had seen the worst of human behavior in his life. Nothing surprised him anymore. The killing had become a way of life for him.

His current target was a high-profile businessman. The man who wanted him dead was from a rival business house. The mercenary seldom looked into the private life of his targets. He planned, set a date, and got on with it. That way, the emotional baggage was kept to a minimum. Not that he cared. He was way beyond that now.

The afternoon sun was bright. The wind speed was accurate and in the right direction. Having trained as a sniper he could easily do the job from 1000 yards away. That is why the hillside farmhouse played a perfect location for his hit of the day. The family was in the lawn, readying for a barbeque. The man in question was at the barbeque tossing the meat which was almost done and ready to be served. Without waiting any further, the mercenary locked his target. The bullet from the Barrett M 82 sniper rifle found its mark. The target never felt the pain when the bullet hit him on his temple. He just collapsed into a pool of blood, to the deafening screams of his near and dear.

His job done, the mercenary quickly gathered his gear, and without any fuss cleared the area driving away as fast as he could.

Chapter 1

Susheela Jaganathan was up every single day at 4 am. It is not that she couldn't sleep. It is just that her job demanded that she get up early if she had to find time to do the things she wanted to. She was a spinster and she had chosen her path. Nothing mattered more to her than the post she held. Of course, she had risen up the ladder over the years only because of her unapologetic and complete devotion to her work. It was very tiresome stressful and quite lonely at the top. Nevertheless, she hardly deterred.

Her routine, every single day, would begin with an hour of meditation and yoga. That done, she would spend an hour in the spacious garden walking her way through the numerous plants and clearing her mind to deal with the day's problems. A light breakfast followed that, after which she would be ready for the day.

This morning was no different. Breakfast was done, and Susheela took an hour to get ready. As the clock showed 8.30 am she was ready and out the front door. An array of cars was waiting for her. She got into the designated one and was quickly whisked away to her workplace. Reaching her destination, she stepped out of the car, to be followed by her secretary and other dignitaries. Taking powerful strides, she finally entered a room already occupied by the other ministers of her cabinet. Madam Susheela Jaganathan, the leader of a nation of more than a billion people, was ready for another day of dealing with her country's problems.

Around the same time, yet another closed-door meeting was in progress not very far from where the honorable Prime Minister was in session. This meeting had all the bigwigs of the country's intelligence agencies, anti-terrorism squads, and the like .. Their agenda was how to deal with the many threats to the life of their Prime Minister who was going to embark on a massive election rally touring the entire nation over the coming months, wherein, she would be the most vulnerable.

Chapter 2

"Good morning David saab ". said Vijay as he barged into the room in his attempt to wake up the sole occupant of the one-bed studio. It was only around 7am of a glorious spring morning. The mercenary was still in bed. In his current avatar people knew him as David King from Australia. To them, he was a businessman who dealt with recycling of electronic waste. He had come to the capital city of this vast country and set up his home and business over the last 2 months. He told his acquaintances that he was on a business trip and would probably stay for a year in the country. Vijay knew him for most of the last 2 months. He helped him with things. He was a young lad of 16 and did these odd jobs to pay for his school tuition. He wanted to become a pilot at some point and was working hard for it. He never missed school and studies. The mercenary liked him for his sincerity, although he kept any conversation with him to a minimum. It helped that Vijay was very good at English. "Good morning Vijay" he replied, waking up to the call. "What do you want for breakfast? Saab? Today is Sunday. Do you want anything special?" enquired Vijay. "No. Just the usual. Make it quick please. I want to visit the Parliament House today" he replied. "Oh. It's a beautiful place, Saab" added Vijay. "Let's not waste more time then, "said David and walked into the shower.

......

Shortly after breakfast, the mercenary reached the parliament House. He had been scouting the area and also the other places that were frequented by his next target over many days since his arrival. He had received the call while on a break from his last job. That surprised him. He usually preferred to lie low for a few months after a job. However, the client had been convincing and the money promised was huge. It was only by knowing who his target was that he realized it was not going to be easy. Albeit the perils he had packed his bags and left for his destination. He was in the country for about two months now and was still not sure how he could execute his plan. At times he felt the task would be easier in a place other than the capital. The security detail in the capital was very tight and he hadn't got the hang of it one hundred percent. He was aware the country was getting ready for elections. He hoped the window of opportunity would present itself very soon. Walking around for about an hour he made some notes and returned to his apartment.

As he entered, he saw Vijay preparing his lunch while listening to some music. Instantly he became chatty. "Ah. You are back. Lunch will be ready soon. You know Saab. In a fortnight it will be Holi. It is a big festival of colors in our country. All the people play with colors and celebrate brotherhood and love. This Holi, our school will have a grand celebration. We have a very important guest coming. Our honorable Prime Minister. Madame is very happy with the progress our government school has made in education and she is coming to honor us. It's going to be a great day for all of us." an elated Vijay informed David. The mercenary couldn't believe what he was hearing. He went up to Vijay, put his arm around his shoulder, and said " Oh really. I would love to visit your school, Vijay".

Chapter 3

Vijay was very excited to show David Saab the Holi preparations in his school. He couldn't believe that David Saab wanted to visit his school too. It was a Monday morning. Shortly after breakfast the two of them took the metro to reach the school.

As they reached the gates a group of boys greeted Vijay and David. David kept a low profile talking very little. He could feel the buzz all over. Vijay kept chatting all along while showing him the various activities that were getting readied for the visit of the country's Prime Minister. It was exactly two weeks from now.

David kept nodding his head as if listening ardently. However, far from it, he was making a mental note of the school's layout, the surroundings, and the security personnel who were already in good numbers and patrolling all over. He could see new CCTV cameras being installed. Trying to identify a vantage point for the stage that was being set, David excused himself and started walking around the compound. The school building was surrounded on three sides by other concrete structures. The stage being erected overlooked a large playground that bordered onto a small hillock. It was almost 500 meters away. Although it was plain grassland David couldn't think of a better place for his kill. He decided to check it out the next day. Finding his way back to where he had left Vijay, David joined him. Vijay introduced him to his school principal. David kept his conversation to a minimum and decided to leave. He had seen enough without making it seem obvious and suspicious.

Chapter 4

David was alone in his apartment. He was done with his breakfast and getting ready to go. Vijay had left for school. In the quiet of the morning, his thoughts were racing towards his goal. It was a good two months since he was on his current mission. Nowhere near achieving it. He went through the visit to Vijay's school and recreated the scene mentally. "Would you like to come with me today too, David Saab.?" Vijay had asked. " No Vijay. I am busy today. Also, I won't be in for lunch. Don't wait for me". He replied. He did not want to be seen again with the boy. It was time. He had to plan it in the next few days.

....

Madame Susheela Ranganathan began her day with a meeting arranged by her security team. Her next major public event in the capital was the Holi celebrations at a government school. The chief security advisor was very anxious about the whole thing. " Madam, it is still not too late to cancel the event. It is a very vulnerable situation you are putting yourself into." He requested. " I will hear nothing more of that. I am not going to cancel it at any cost. It is very dear to my heart. You do your job and I will do mine" she replied, concluding the meeting.

......

With the prime Minister now confirming her presence at the school event, more meetings were held and many decisions were taken. Passes would be given to all the attendees. Parents of the children would not be allowed into the premises. The canine team would be deployed all around to look for any hidden dangers. The road leading to the school would be cordoned off for at least a kilometer with appropriate traffic diversions. Slowly things were getting under control.

....

David left home to finalize things. He got off the metro and took the bus to reach his destination. The last mile was a difficult climb to the top of the hillock. It seemed plain and devoid of anyone or anything. A few cows were grazing. Other than that, he was on his own. The sun was quite high in the day and the atmosphere was dry. The wind speed was to a minimum. Choosing a vantage point he looked in the direction of the school. It was a good 500 meters away. With his binoculars, he could see that hardly anything stood between him and the stage. It would do. He had to find a means of transport for a quick getaway. He made a note to do that at the earliest and walked away.

The next morning David excused himself after breakfast and left home to do some more planning.

Chapter 5

The bright and beautiful spring morning announced the arrival of a grand Holiday in the capital. Vijay was up at 4 am. He was in the kitchen trying to finish things as quickly as he could. After all, it was the day he had been waiting for. The students were all requested to be at school by 6 am. The security over the last week was so beefed up that even going to class was a task, with numerous security checks made at numerous points, within the campus. The students were told not to carry any bags on that day. They were given fresh identity cards, each one was instructed to carry them at all times. Vijay made breakfast and woke David to tell him he was leaving and said his goodbyes. David had told him a week ago that he would be leaving the capital that day and very soon, the country as well, for, his work was almost done. Vijay was sad that David would be gone when he came back but he knew that someday that would happen.

David readied himself too. He packed all his stuff and left after breakfast. He wanted this done and be gone. It had not been easy. He went to the metro station where he had hired a locker. He opened it and deposited all his stuff, took the metro, and got down two stations away. During his many outings, he found a dilapidated building in the neighborhood of this metro. Making sure no one really used the building by repeatedly keeping a watch on the premises he had hidden his weapons there. All of these weapons he had smuggled into the country many days prior and various sources. He collected them and walked his way to a nearby inconspicuous garage from where he had hired the vehicle for his getaway. He had paid a lot of money to get the vehicle without giving him many documents. By the time he got into the vehicle and was on his way, it was almost 7 am. It would take him an hour to get there. The target was expected to arrive at 9.30 am.

....

Madame Prime Minister was as usual out of her home at 8.30 am. She considered the day as any other. For her security detail, however, it was going to be nerve -wrecking three hours before she was in the safety of secure surroundings.

.....

The school campus was already buzzing with a lot of activity. The security was so tight that children were afraid to move around. The principal was overseeing last-minute arrangements. The stage was well decorated. The school band was ready and - waiting at the entrance. A large pandal was in place. A cutout of the Prime Minister stood proud by the entrance. The security was making sure every single person was following the protocol dictated to them. It was time. Half an hour of the Prime Minister's presence in the school had cost more than three months of planning.

......

The motor cavalcade made its way to the school campus. Almost a kilometer from the school, public traffic was diverted and the roads were cordoned off from the public. Policemen stood on either side of the newly paved roads in sheer attention. People thronged on either side of the road to catch a glimpse of their beloved leader.

....

David made his way to the pre-selected vantage point. He parked his vehicle not very far from his reach. He noticed that in the quiet of the morning hours ,no one was around. That played to his advantage. Binoculars in hand he scanned the area and felt reassured that nothing could go wrong. Armed with his carefully chosen weapon he was ready and patiently waited for the right time.

......

Madame Prime Minister alighted to the chorus of the school band that started playing instantly. A very young pupil presented her with a bouquet of flowers and welcomed her in. Her party representative of the constituency was also very much present to welcome her. The principal and other teachers walked with her to the podium. She was quite pleased with all the arrangements and conveyed the same to the school head. No sooner than she was seated in the podium along with a few dignitaries, the carefully crafted day's events began. A prayer song started the program, followed by a short detail of the school's achievements. A few students were presented with medals from the Prime Minister for various outstanding achievements. For them, it was a moment they would cherish for life. Finally, the mike was handed to the Prime Minister. As she stood up and walked towards the mike her security immediately became alert and covered her from all sides. Madame Prime Minister started her speech to pin drop silence.

....

David was all attention. He was waiting for this very moment. He readied himself and his gun to get a clear view of the target. The wind speed was accurate and it was a clear field. He pulled the trigger and felt the bullet spring toward the target.

....

The Prime Minister was well into her speech. She was conveying her good wishes to the school and said the school is a role model for the other schools of the country to emulate. Suddenly there was a commotion. Out of nowhere a boy about ten years sprang toward the stage and her. Before the security could stop him, he was on the stage and fell at her feet. Madame Prime Minister immediately stooped down to pick up the boy. At that very moment, someone heard a thud and one of the security personnel was on the floor, blood pouring through his arm. A few moments of stunned silence filled the air. Without another minute wasted the commandos quickly surrounded the Prime Minister and whisked her to the car and were off. The others were left behind to wonder what went wrong. The medical team that were already there, rushed to the wounded man and tended to him. Soon there was chaos, panic, and confusion all over.

......

David couldn't believe what happened. For the first time in a very long time, things had gone wrong. He had missed. There was nothing he could change now. Without wasting time, he packed his gear and sprinted toward his getaway vehicle and was off. He had some brainstorming to do.

Chapter 6

Two months later

After waking up to the shocking news of the assassination attempt on their beloved leader, the entire country was looking for answers. The stray bullet was found and sent for forensic studies. Meetings were held amongst various national security agencies on how to tighten the apparent loopholes in the security detail of the Prime Minister. The world was shocked too and poured in their voice of detest and concern. The school authorities continued to attend regular briefings with the security agencies to look for anything that may throw light on the events of the day. So far it remained largely elusive. Vijay had come home shocked. He wanted to tell it all to David but unfortunately, David had left as planned. He hoped he would hear from David sometime soon.

Madame Prime Minister was unaffected by the fiasco and continued with her life and job as before. She was well aware that constant threats to her life came with her job but it did not stop her from doing what she had to. However, she followed basic protocol as ordered by her security to avoid alarming situations. The elections were aroundthe corner and she had a lot of public appearances to make.

Meanwhile, David had moved to the south of the country and now lived under a new alias. He had chosen the place based on the forthcoming itinerary of his target, who would soon be there to inaugurate the new golden dome dedicated to the town's main temple. The temple itself was a massive architectural and engineering marvel built completely out of stone seven centuries ago by the then-kings. The entire town thrived on the activities of that temple. He was always on the lookout for someone coming in to arrest him, but to his surprise, it had not happened so far. He kept to himself and moved around inconspicuously gathering whatever information from the locals about the most awaited event of their town.

Chapter 7

David woke up to a very rainy morning. Seasons had changed indicating the passage of time. The region of the country he currently lived in was experiencing monsoons and cooling the sweltering heat. He had a light breakfast and made his way to the temple complex. The day in question was now just two months away. He had planned a few things and always made it a point to visit the temple premises every day now. To people who spoke to him, he told them he was from a magazine and was writing a series about the magnificent temples of India.

"Vanakkam sir", Annachi, the fruit seller, greeted David. "Vanakkam",David replied. "Coffee acha," the man probed. ``oh yes oh yes'' David said and moved away. He had picked up the local language a little and was able to understand quite a bit. With the camera in hand, he was trying to capture something when suddenly there was a commotion. He saw a boy of ten running in his direction, and a lady chasing him shouting "nilludaa," adi vanguve." As the lady crossed David she turned to look him in the eye. David felt his head spinning the moment he saw her. She was a vision. Her jet-black tresses were left open, and they danced in the wind as she turned to look at him. Her eyes were a piercing blue complimenting a face the color of honey. She was probably in her twenties. He couldn't believe what he was seeing. For a fleeting moment, the lady smiled at him as if teasing him and continued in her pursuit of the boy. David ran after her for a short distance and then stopped. But his heart was racing and against all his principles he kept telling himself he had to find her.

....

It was a couple of days after that incident. David was scouting around the temple area hoping he would see the lady again. He had asked around but no one was able to tell him anything. He couldn't take her off his mind. That was so very unusual for him. At that very moment, he saw the same little boy once again. He couldn't believe his eyes. He ran towards him, caught hold of him, and started a conversation. "Hello young lad. What is your name? Do you speak English?" He asked. " Hello. What do you want?" asked the boy perturbed that some stranger and that too a foreigner had cornered him. "Oh no, don't worry. I am not going to harm you. What is your name and do you speak English? "David spoke slowly and loudly hoping the boy would understand." Yes, I know English. I study in an English school. My name is Karthikeyan". "Karthi what?" queried David. "Karthikeyan" but you can call me Karthi.. What do you want?" He asked again. Just then David heard her voice. "Thambi" she called out to the boy." Ennada pannerae? What are you doing?" As she saw David holding him she was aghast and came quickly to set him free. David was mesmerised once again. She was wearing a beautiful blue saree with Jasmine in her hair, her lips red with the betel nut she was chewing. The eyes piercing him, she started talking to David in her native language with her brother translating for them."Why are you holding my brother and what do you want?" " Oh no please don't be worried. I was just trying to make friends with him". said David. "We don't need new friends," she said." We have to go.

Come Karthi. Don't waste my time. Amma is waiting. Lunch is ready" she called out to him.". Wait, t wait, please " pleaded David. "What is it?" she queried. "I am writing about this glorious temple. Will you help me with it?". he asked. "How can I help you?". "By showing me things that are not known to the common tourist. Please just for a day". David was almost on his knees now. She looked annoyingly at him, looked at her brother, and said "Ask him to be here at 5 in the evening. And tell him only today and only with you around.".David thanked her profusely and before she left dared to ask her name. She turned back, once again sweeping him off his feet, and said "Selvi.." and walked away.

....

David couldn't wait for it to be 5 in the evening. He was dressed in traditional ethnic clothes, something he had learned to wear during his stay. He looked dapper and was at the spot where he had left them at the stroke of five. His waiting was soon rewarded. Selvi and Karthi made their way toward him. He couldn't take his eyes off her. She looked elegant in a simple davani,a spin-off of the saree. Always with flowers in her hair, she looked ethereal. Having greeted him she immediately asked him to follow her and started explaining to him the history of the temple from her perspective. All along she spoke in her native language with the brother translating it for her. To David, it did not matter what was being said. He was like a lamb following her in rapt attention. How could he have come to this state? The committed hour went by like a breeze.

Very soon it was time for them to go. David made her promise they would meet him again the next day at the same time.

Chapter 8

It was almost six weeks since their first meeting. David and Selvi had grown to like each other. They spent many hours in each other's company. David wanted to protect Selvi all the time. She was such a gentle person, always looking out for other people and helping them. He had visited their modest home several times by now. They lived a kilometer away from the temple. Her father had a small condiment shop and Selvi helped him there. She had told him that she stopped her studies after the 10th grade. She also told him that the boy was not her real brother and she had come to this town only a few months ago looking for a job. She was an orphan, and the boy's family was kind enough to give her shelter. The family's hopes were on the boy whom they made sure got a decent education.

David and Selvi became the talk of the town. Her foster parents were initially very worried but Selvi put them at ease and assured them that she would always be the dutiful daughter. The couple had learned to understand each other without the boy's help, with Selvi trying to learn English and teaching David some Tamizh. Some evenings she would spend time in David's home, cooking delicious Indian food. It was as if David was living a dream. He knew what he was in the country for and also that entailed putting her life in danger too. Many times,she would stay back with him, completely surrendering to his gentle advances. Their lovemaking was surreal after which he would draw out his plan on the computer with her sitting beside him. She would ask him what he was working on and his reply was always vague.. Not that she cared. She knew he was doing something very important.

One such night they were sitting on the balcony of his home. It was close to midnight. A gentle breeze filled the air and a full moon lit the sky. Selvi had completely taken over the act of making love just an hour ago and David was soaking in that experience. Suddenly Selvi asked, "Will you leave me and go?" David was shocked. The gravity of that question shook him. It brought him back to his senses and his purpose. It was only two weeks now before his target was coming to town for a very important public function. He knew what he had to do and over the days planned it as well. Meeting and falling in love with Selvi was the only thing that was not in his scheme of things. He had no regrets though. He went up to her, lovingly held her face in his hands, and said "You know I will have to leave the country very soon. We have talked about that. But I will definitely come back for you." And without another moment lost he asked "Will you marry me Selvi?"

Selvi couldn't believe what she was hearing. She jumped and hugged him, crying all the while and shouting "Yes. yes. yes"

Chapter 9

After David's proposal things had moved pretty fast. Selvi had gone home and broken the news to her family. Her parents couldn't believe what was happening. David was clear that he would leave the country after the wedding. He had conveyed this to Selvi and her family. He would come back to take Selvi with him some time . They agreed to that although there really was no other option.

The town was preparing for a great event in a week's time. The Prime Minister of the country was coming. Security personnel were coming in from various parts of the country. They had bomb squads, dog squads,army, gentry, and whatnot. Moving around the temple premises was becoming extremely difficult.

Selvi wanted the wedding on the same day as the event. This irked David a bit. Rather than disappoint her, he agreed only if it could happen much before sunrise. It would be a very small affair with only her family. David had told them he had something very important to attend after that and would be back only the following day. Shortly after which he would leave the country. Selvi had chosen the venue. It was a good twenty miles away from the main temple. It was also a small temple on a hillock. The wedding would be around 4 am.

The previous day David packed his luggage and everything else he needed to get away quickly. He loaded his vehicle and made sure everything was accounted for.

Finally, it was happening. He woke up early and hoped Selvi was up and getting ready too. He had zeroed in on his spot for his job and was confident he would do it this time. For the first time he was tense. Too many things happening all at once. He got into his vehicle and headed for the temple hoping all would be fine. As he was driving he could see security personnel all over. Random checking was happening. He stopped at a signal when a policeman came up to his vehicle. He signaled him to roll down his window. David did that with a lot of aapprehensions, his heart racing. "Hello, sir. Where are you going so early in the morning? You know this is a no-go zone. Please turn back. Oh, I am so sorry" David apologized and quickly turned back rather than argue. He had to now take a longer route. By the time he reached his destination Selvi and her family were waiting for him. He parked his vehicle and started walking towards them when he heard the sirens and saw three police cars moving towards the temple. He saw the horror on Selvi's face. He ran to her, held her hand and started running to the temple sanctum all the time protecting her. Her family was aghast as they heard the police call out his name, and tell him to drop on his knees. Selvi screamed not knowing what was happening. As the police closed in on them he looked her in the eye and said "Forgive me Selvi but I have to do this now "and pulled out his gun ready to aim at the police. "You can never be forgiven, "said Selvi in perfect English as she plunged the dagger she had carried with her into his heart. A perplexed David slumped before her not ever knowing what just happened.

The chief of the country's top security agency stepped out of one of the vehicles and walked toward Selvi. As soon as he came close to her she stood in attention, saluting him and said "Special Officer Aarthi Subramaniam at your service Sir."

The chief shook her hands and said "Well done, Aarthi. Mission accomplished."

Lying there in a pool of blood was the unknown Assassin.

Epilogue

The very same day, Madame Prime Minister conducted her public function in the temple town to an exhilarating audience with a lot of fanfare and adulation.

After the first attempt on the Prime Minister's life, a special task force of trained and Elite officers was appointed in the country and sent to various regions of the land. They were all extensively trained in commando operations, ruthless, and capable of handling any situation with ease. Their mission was to keep their eyes and ears open for any news that may be of use in the search for the elusive Assassin. No one even knew of their existence except a select core group in the country's top security agency. Special Officer Aarthi Subramaniam was one of the team. She was well known for her ability to integrate into the milieu and camouflage well. She was assigned to the temple town where a very important event was to take place. She had somehow adopted the boy's family and was on her mission from day one. Very soon she met the Assassin and found her way into his life. Constantly in touch with her bosses, she had completely plotted the entire plan leading up to the encounter at the temple. The few onlookers who witnessed the event were quietly whisked away and counseled.

The body of the Assassin was briskly disposed of without much ado. There was no press meet and no announcements made regarding the same, at any time after the event.

Special Officer Aarthi Subramaniam was duly appreciated for her courage and bravery in the closed-door meeting of the office of the nation's topmost security agency.

Madame Prime Minister was briefed about the recent developments. She congratulated the team on their ability to take down the man.

For her and the rest of the country, it was business as usual.

About the Book

"Dr. Latha, in her collection of seven short stories, has really created a ripple in bringing out excellent stories with intrigue, mysteries, and twists. It catches one by the lapel and pulls them through till the end without a pause!"

– Prof. S. Venkateswaran

"Dr. Latha Venkateswaran, an eminent pediatric surgeon has revealed yet another facet of her multi-talented personality – this time her literary skills are mirrored in this collection of six short stories. She weaves magic through her heart-warming tales of human emotions, love, and compassion. While her stories chug along smoothly, a gut-wrenching twist at the end suddenly takes you on an emotional roller coaster reflecting painful realities witnessed in everyday life. A superb effort!"

– S. Subramaniam

Dy. Inspector General, SSB, Ministry of Home Affairs

"When you want a break in your routine or when you want a spark in your mundane life, I would urge you to pick up this book and read a story it will definitely ignite your brain and make you wonder and ruminate!"

Dr. Archana Bilagi

"Ripples contains a marvellous range of short stories that delight and surprise equally. Like any good story, the broad outlines of many of the stories and the sense of the unexpected twist in the tale will stay in your mind long after you finish the book."

– Dr. Varsha RK

"Ripples is a collection of intriguing short stories each with a nail-biting twist. The author pays attention to great detail that keeps the reader fully engrossed!"

Dr. S. Raveendran

"Dr Latha's stories are truly thrilling and give one the experience of being on a roller coaster with all the twists and turns - even with sudden 90° drops! I really enjoyed each story and used to wait for the next one - wondering how she could possibly top the previous one and she always did."

– Mrs. Parvathy Narayanaswamy

"Dr. Latha carries out her profession and passion with equal ease and Elan! Ripples is a collection of Dr. Latha's succinct stories. Her writing style entwines the reader with the lead characters and it's only when you're done reading you realise you live in a different world!"

– Dr. Aishwarya Subramanian